Paper Bird

Paper Bird

Arcadio Lobato

with illustrations by Emilio Urberuaga

Carolrhoda Books, Inc./Minneapolis

In a beautiful city there lived an artist. He was working
late into the night one night to make a birthday present
for his little girl.

"I will draw her a bird that's so beautiful and so real,
it will fly," the artist said to himself as his pen and
paintbrush flew across the paper.

When at last he had finished the drawing, the artist
stretched and sighed and went to bed. Only the cat
was left in the room, and she, too, was ready to sleep.
But just as she curled into a ball and began to dream,
the cat was awakened by a small voice.

"I can't fly! I can't fly!" it said. (It was the artist's
new picture lying on the table.)

Slowly and sleepily the cat opened one eye.

"Of course you can't fly," the cat grumbled. "You are
a paper bird. Now be quiet so I can get some sleep."

"But I have to fly," the bird cried. "The artist said
so. Can't you help me?"

By now the cat was rather annoyed. She didn't like
to be bothered just when she had curled up into a cozy
little ball to sleep. So without another word, the cat
took the paper and threw it out the window. Then
she curled up once more and went back to her dreams.

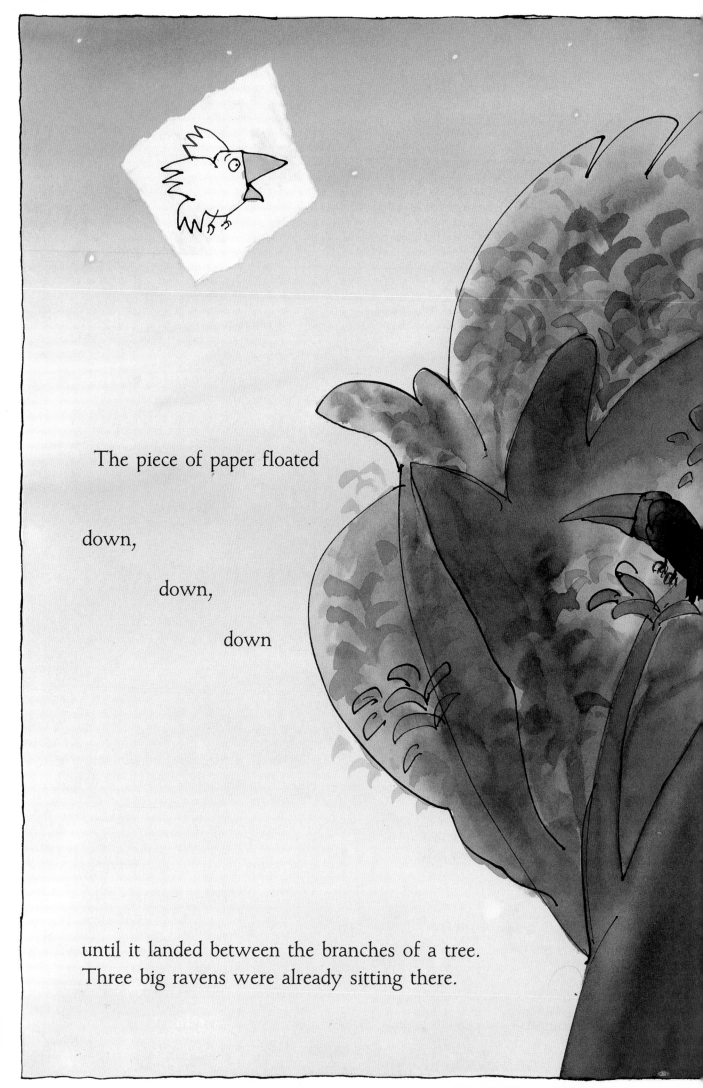

The piece of paper floated

down,

    down,

        down

until it landed between the branches of a tree.
Three big ravens were already sitting there.

"I flew! I flew!" exclaimed the paper bird.

"So what," said one of the ravens. "I fly every day."

"Who's making all that racket?" complained another.

"I'm a bird and I'm just learning how to fly," explained the paper bird. "I already know how to fly down. Now all I have to do is learn how to fly up."

The ravens didn't know what to make of that.

"A paper bird! And one that can talk!" said one.

"How very strange," said another.

The three ravens talked and talked among themselves until finally they announced:

"O Honorable, Miraculous Bird, we are simple ravens and do not know about such things as talking paper birds. But if you wish, we can take you to the owl. She's very wise and will certainly help you."

One of the ravens carried the paper bird high above the owl's perch and then let go. While floating

down,

down,

down,

the paper bird called out, "Owl! Oh, Owl, can you help me? I want to learn how to fly. I can already fly down, but how can I fly up?"

The owl looked the paper bird over carefully, and then she said, "I can see that you are a very unusual case. You're not a bird, but you *are* a drawing of a bird. And you can talk! Hmmm.... This is very unusual.... Perhaps you are a magic bird."

"You are very wise indeed," the paper bird said. "But tell me, can you help me or not?"

"Certainly," the owl replied. "I'll take you to the swallows. If anyone knows anything about flying, the swallows do. And just now they're teaching their children to fly. If you pay close attention, you may learn to fly, too."

"Wonderful!" shouted the paper bird, and he was very happy.

Up on the roof, the whole swallow family was ready for their first flying lesson. The owl dropped the paper bird from her beak and flew away.

"Will you teach me how to fly?" asked the paper bird, as he floated

down,

down,

down.

"With pleasure!" answered the swallows.

But although they tried very hard to teach the paper bird to fly, the swallows did not succeed. Again and again they carried him up to the highest tower and pushed him off the roof. The paper bird floated easily to the ground but could never fly up.

"It's no use," the paper bird sobbed. "I'll never learn how to fly."

"Don't cry," the swallows said comfortingly. "We're just country birds, and you were born in the city. Perhaps city birds fly differently. We'll carry you to the city birds and see what they can do for you."

And so they flew to the beautiful city. Over the high rooftops, sparrows and swifts were flying in circles.

"Hey, you over there, you city birds," the country swallows called, "we've got a very special case for you. Our friend here wants to fly, but he just can't seem to learn how."

The city birds took one look at the paper bird and said, "But hold on! That's not a real bird at all! That's art! Art's very important, but it belongs on walls in people's houses. Humans look at art and say, 'How beautiful!' or 'It looks so real it even seems to be alive,' but they don't expect it to fly. Art is never really alive. So, you see, this paper bird will never fly."

"Ohhhh," said the swallows sadly, for they knew the paper bird would be very unhappy at this news. Then, in a great gust of wind, the piece of paper fluttered off the roof and floated

   down,

     down,

       down

         toward the ground.

"So I'm a work of art and not a bird after all," the paper bird said to himself with a sigh as he floated away. "I wonder what I'm good for. The ravens, the owl, the sparrows, and the swifts can all fly up and down, wherever they want. Here I am, a bird who's just a drawing of a bird and trapped in a prison of paper at that!"

While the paper bird floated down and thought these very sad thoughts, some cats rounded a corner and looked up in surprise. "A talking piece of paper! How odd!" they all cried—all except for the artist's cat, who knew the paper bird at once, took him in her mouth, and carried him carefully back to the artist's house.

"I'm sorry, bird," said the cat. "It wasn't right of me to throw you out the window like that. But I don't like to be bothered when I'm trying to sleep."

"I'll forgive you," the paper bird replied. "Thanks to you, I went on a great journey and made many friends. I will always think of them when I am hanging up on a wall, all alone in my picture frame."

The cat wanted to answer, but just then the artist came into the room, whistling happily.

He took some glue, some string, some tacks, and some sticks...

...and he made a present for his daughter—a beautiful kite decorated with a work of art, the paper bird!

And so the paper bird's wish came true. He flew! He floated
        down,
                down,
                        down.

                                up.
                        up,
                up,
And better still—he flew

He glided happily in the air, and all his friends came to say hello.

"I'm so happy to be a work of art!" he shouted out
to them. "And one that can fly, too!"

This edition first published 1994 by Carolrhoda Books, Inc.

Original edition published in 1993 by Bohem Press under the title *Der Papiervogel.* Copyright © 1993 Bohem Press, Zurich, Switzerland.

Carolrhoda Books, Inc. c/o The Lerner Group
241 First Avenue North, Minneapolis, MN 55401

Library of Congress Cataloging-in-Publication Data

Lobato, Arcadio.
  [Papiervogel. English]
  Paper bird / Arcadio Lobato ; with illustrations by Emilio Urberuaga.
    p. cm.
  Summary: A drawing of a bird tries without success to learn to fly,
until the artist completes his original design and makes flight possible for it.
  ISBN 0-87614-817-8 (lib. bdg.)
  [1. Birds—Fiction. 2. Flight—Fiction. 3. Art—Fiction. 4. Kites—Fiction.]
I. Urberuaga, Emilio, ill. II. Title.
PZ7.L7788Pap 1994
[E]—dc20   93-24469
                                          CIP
                                          AC

Printed in Italy by Grafiche AZ, Verona
Bound in the United States of America

1 2 3 4 5 6 – I/OS – 99 98 97 96 95 94